CAMPFIRE CRISIS

by
Blake Hoena

Minneapolis, Minnesota

Dedication

To my Grandpa and Grandma Hoena—thanks for teaching me the joys of camping.

Original concept by Blake Hoena and Ryan Jacobson
Edited by Dana Kuznar
Artwork by Shane Nitzsche

10 9 8 7 6 5 4 3 2 1

Library of Congress Control Number: 2012922814

ISBN: 978-0-9883662-5-1

How to Use This Book

Read each chapter, just like a normal book. You will come to a page with big, black arrows. That means it's time to make a choice. Pick one of the options, and follow its arrow to the next paragraph. Read that paragraph. If you made the right choice, go to the next page. If you made the wrong choice, pick again.

Cast of Characters

You—the reader. This is your adventure.

Carla—one of your best friends. She's sporty and loves to be outdoors. She enjoys camping and hiking. She is probably the best soccer player at school.

Mike—one of your best friends. He has some allergies and likes video games more than sports. He is one of the smartest kids in your class. Mike is really good with maps.

1. Going Camping

You skip up the stairs, two steps at a time. Your parents just told you some great news. You can't wait to share it with your friends.

Carla and Mike are in your bedroom. They look up as you burst through the door.

"Well?" says Carla.

"What did they say?" Mike asks.

Your friends sit on the bedroom floor. Camping gear is spread out around them.

"We can have our own campsite!" you shout.

"All right! Cool!" they say, sounding excited.

You and your friends are good campers. You have gone on many camping trips with your parents. Usually, you share a campsite with the grown-ups.

This time will be different. Your parents are letting you have your own site. You'll pack your own gear. You'll pitch your own tent. It will be exciting to camp on your own.

"My parents will be in the campsite next to ours," you add. You're glad they will be close, in case you need help. After all, you'll be in the middle of the woods.

Your parents will bring the tents. They'll also pack most of the food and cooking gear. But you're bringing your own snacks. You already have them packed in a bag. You have some dried fruit and trail mix. And, of course, marshmallows and graham crackers for s'mores. The chocolate bars are in your parents' cooler.

You each have a sleeping bag rolled up. There are three flashlights. You each have a utility tool with a screwdriver, scissors, and small saw.

"Remember," you say. "We have to carry our gear to the campsite. So only take what you need."

"What about these?" Carla asks.

In one hand, she holds her hand-crank radio. It has a lever that turns, which charges the battery.

With the radio, you can listen to music whenever you want. You can also get weather reports.

In her other hand, Carla holds her smart phone. The phone won't work in the woods where you're going. But it still has games. If rain comes, you and your friends can stay in your tent and play.

Which one will you tell Carla to pack?

The hand-crank radio

The smart phone

The hand-crank radio: You tell Carla to pack her radio. Good choice! It doesn't have any games, but it will always have power. You just crank its lever. Then you can listen to music. You can also get weather reports if it looks stormy outside.

The smart phone: You tell Carla to pack her phone. It would be fun to play games. But the phone will run out of power. You won't be able to recharge it. And what if a storm comes? You might need to hear weather reports. You should tell Carla to pack the radio instead.

"Aw, man," Carla says. "I was hoping to beat the next level on *Zombie Zoo*."

"Did you get to the monkey zombies yet?" Mike asks.

"No," Carla says. "But I suppose my phone wouldn't be very fun once it ran out of power." She sets her phone aside and packs the radio.

The three of you gather the rest of your gear. You each have rain ponchos, an extra pair of warm clothes, and water sandals. You can wear the sandals while exploring the nearby river with your parents.

When your backpacks are full, you take your gear downstairs. Your parents help you put everything into the car.

Now you're ready. You just need to wait for tomorrow morning, when it's time to leave.

Carla says, "Let's play *Zombie Zoo* before bed."

You and Mike like that idea. The three of you run back upstairs to play.

2. Setting Up

The next morning, your parents wake you very early.

"Can we rest a little longer?" Mike whines.

Carla sits up and rubs her eyes. "I didn't get much sleep," she says. "I kept dreaming about those penguin zombies."

You put a baseball cap over your messy hair, and you leap out of bed. You're excited to get to the campground. "Let's have some breakfast," you tell your friends.

You each gulp down a bowl of cereal. When the dishes are cleaned, you crawl into the backseat of your parents' car. You're finally on your way. You'll be camping at a state park, many miles from home. The drive is several hours long.

By the time you arrive at the park, you're antsy. You scramble to get out of the car. You stretch as your mom checks in at the visitor center.

Your dad helps you get ready for the hike to your campsite. It's about a mile from where you park. You grab your backpack and sling it over your shoulders. Your dad straps your sleeping bag to it. He helps your friends do the same.

Your mom returns. "Is everyone ready?"

You pick up the bag of snacks. Carla and Mike each grab a jug of water. This hike will be the hardest part of the trip. Your gear is heavy, but you nod.

Your dad takes the lead. He disappears into the woods. You follow him. Next come Carla and Mike. Your mom goes last.

The trail winds its way toward your campsite. Sometimes it follows the river. Other times the trail goes through thick forests.

With all the gear, you're tired and sweaty when you arrive.

There are three campsites near each other. They are connected by narrow trails. Your parents take one site. You, Mike, and Carla take another. You see that a tent is set up in the third campsite. But you don't see any people there.

After your dad sets down his gear, he brings your tent to you. "Before any exploring," he says, "you need to set up your campsite."

"Okay, Dad," you reply.

The three of you unload your gear and plop it down. You and Mike work together to set up your tent. You've done it plenty of times before, so it doesn't take long.

Once all your gear is in the tent, Carla asks, "What should I do with our snacks?"

You could put them in your tent. You're only going to be gone for a little while, but you'll be

hungry when you get back. The snacks will be easy to reach.

You also have some rope in your gear. You could hang the bag from a tree branch, away from your campsite. That way, no one else can take it.

What will you do with your snacks?

Put the snacks in your tent.

Hang the snacks from a tree branch.

Put the snacks in your tent: Carla shoves the bag into your tent. But as you're about to leave, you see a squirrel dart across the ground. You don't know what other animals might be in these woods. You don't want them to get at the food in your tent. You should hang the snacks from a tree.

Hang the snacks from a tree branch: You ask Carla to loop the rope over a tree branch. You tie one end of the rope around the bag. You tug on the other end to lift the bag high into the air. Then you tie the rope to another branch. Your food is safe. If wild animals happen to smell it, they won't be able to reach it.

Your mom comes over. She looks up at the bag of food hanging from the tree. She smiles proudly. "Good idea," she says. "Raccoons and bears live around here. You don't want them sniffing around your tent."

She holds out a small canvas sack. It has a red plus sign on the side. "You have your own campsite," she says. "You'll need your own survival kit. It includes a first-aid kit, matches, a flashlight, and other important items."

You go and put it inside your tent, next to the door. That way, it will be easy to find if you need it.

"Your dad and I are going to get some firewood," she says. "Stay together. Stay safe. And stay away from the river."

3. Campfire

You run off to explore with your friends. The three of you hike down the trail. You go all the way back to the visitor center. There, you find out that you can rent canoes and kayaks. They even have fishing poles if you want to go fishing.

Before you leave, Mike grabs a park map. He folds it and stuffs it into his back pocket.

You stop by the playground. You say, "hi," to a few kids your own age. And you play a quick game of tag. Then you hike back.

By the time you get there, your parents have a fire going at their site. You eat hot dogs and potato chips. Then you help your parents clean up.

"Is it time for s'mores?" Mike asks.

You turn to your parents. Your mom nods.

"Yay!" you all cheer.

Mike runs to your campsite to get the bag of snacks. You and Carla search the nearby woods for fallen sticks to roast marshmallows. Then you, Mike, and Carla sit down around the fire.

You each pull out your utility tool.

You use the small blade on it to whittle the end of a stick to a point. Now you're ready for s'mores.

The fire crackles as you roast a marshmallow. You create a sandwich with two graham crackers. Inside, chocolate melts against the hot marshmallow. The s'mores are gooey and delicious.

You notice people in the third campsite. They have a fire going too. But it's too dark to tell who they are. You think two people are over there.

You finish your snack, and it's time for bed. You've had a long day. But you have to prepare your campsite first. Mike and Carla go to hang your snacks in the tree.

"Is there anything you're forgetting?" your dad asks. He looks at the fire.

All the sticks and logs have burned down to embers. There aren't any flames. You could leave the fire pit as is. That will make it easy to start a new fire tomorrow.

Or you could dump water over it. That way, the fire will be put out all the way. But then you'll have to go and get more water tomorrow.

What will you do?

Leave the fire pit alone.

Dump water on the fire pit.

Leave the fire pit alone: There aren't any flames. You tell your dad that it's okay to leave it. But then you see an ember crackle. Sparks shoot up. They land on the ground next to some dry leaves. It would be better to dump water on the pit.

Dump water on the fire pit: You get a jug and pour water over the embers. They hiss and steam. Next, you stir them with a stick. As you turn the coals over, you notice they're still red hot. They could start a fire if a spark landed on dry leaves. You pour more water over the embers.

"Good job," your dad says. "Tomorrow night, we'll have the campfire at your site."

You smile proudly as you say goodnight. You head back to your tent. As you crawl inside, you notice the third campsite. Their fire is still blazing, but you don't see any people.

You duck into your tent and zip up the door. You, Mike, and Carla crawl into your sleeping bags for the night.

4. Forest Fire

You don't fall asleep right away. You turn on the hand-crank radio and listen to the weather report. It says there might be rain during the night. But the skies will be sunny tomorrow.

You and your friends talk about plans for the next day. Mike wants to go bird watching. Carla wants to swim. You want to catch a fish. And there are miles of trails to explore.

Mike falls asleep first. You hear his light snores. Then Carla nods off.

Minutes pass. Your eyelids grow heavy. You feel yourself drifting off. But you don't fall asleep. Something is wrong.

You see shadows dancing against the walls of your tent. The light has grown brighter outside. You

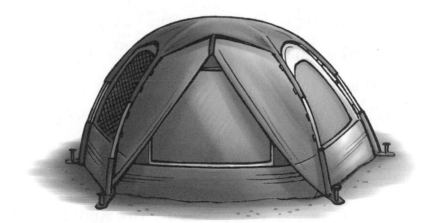

hear an odd crackling sound. It's like hundreds of twigs snapping apart.

You crawl from your sleeping bag and unzip the tent door. When you peek outside, you're amazed at how bright it is. The night has turned dark orange. Then you notice the heat. The forest in front of you is on fire!

"Oh, no!" you shout. "Mike, Carla, get up!"

You jump out of the tent.

"What's going on?" Carla says, rubbing her eyes.

"Come on, guys!" you shout. "Get out of the tent. There's a fire!"

Mike is the first one out. Carla follows. In her hand, she holds the survival kit your mom gave you.

There's a wall of fire between you and your parents' campsite. Flames reach high into the trees.

Will you flee? You only have the clothes that you're wearing. You will need more than that to survive in the woods.

Or will you go back into the tent to grab your gear? It will only take a minute, and you could get some warmer clothes.

What should you do?

Flee.

Grab your gear.

Flee: You tell your friends to get away from the fire. Sparks are flying everywhere. When they land on the ground, the leaves and grass start to smolder. It's best to get safely away from the fire.

Grab your gear: You tell your friends to get their things from the tent. You don't want your stuff to get burned. But sparks are flying everywhere. Some land on your tent. It would be better for you to flee right away.

As you back away from the fire, you hear your parents shouting.

"Head for the visitor center," your dad yells.

"We'll meet you there," your mom shouts.

You now know that you've made the right choice. You should leave your stuff behind.

You turn to your friends. They look frightened. You're scared too, but it's time to move.

"Let's go!" you shout.

5. Lost in the Wild

You run from the flames as fast as you can. Mike is in the lead, then Carla, and finally you.

For the first few minutes, you're on the trail. But soon, branches start whacking you in the arms. You duck under tree limbs and dart around bushes. That doesn't happen on the trail.

Mike suddenly stops. You and Carla almost run into him.

"What is it?" you ask.

He looks down at his feet. "I lost the path."

"That's okay," you say. "The important thing was to get away from the fire. It's pretty dark now. None of us could see the trail."

"Yeah, and we were running fast," Carla adds.

Mike kicks the ground. You can tell he's upset. He's always been good with maps and finding his way around.

"It's nobody's fault," you say. "We ran to safety. That's all."

He looks up and smiles. "I guess you're right" he says.

He seems to feel better. But now you have a new problem. You don't know where you are. And there's not enough light to find the trail.

"What should we do?" Mike asks.

"We're lost," Carla adds.

Your friends look to you.

You have two choices. You could keep walking. Maybe you'll find the trail again.

Or you could stay put. You aren't in any danger from the fire. But you don't know how long it will take for an adult to find you.

What will you do?

Keep going.

Stay where you are.

Keep going: You tell your friends to keep moving. You start walking in the direction you think the trail is. After just five steps, you stop. You aren't sure if you're going in the right direction. It would be better if you stayed put.

Stay where you are: You decide to stay put. You're lost. If you keep moving in the woods, you might move farther from help. You could also stumble over a fallen tree or step into a hole. If you got hurt, you could be in more danger.

You remember what your dad once told you. "If you're lost, stay where you are. It's easier for people to find you."

You and your friends sit down. You notice that Carla is holding the survival kit.

She says. "It was right by the door. I grabbed it when we left the tent." She hands you the kit.

You unzip it to look inside. There are bandages. There's also a small flashlight and a utility tool. There are some wooden matches and a whistle. With everything else, there are three rain ponchos.

6. The River

Carla uses the whistle to call for help. She blows into it as hard as she can. *Tweet! Tweet!*

"Mom! Dad!" you shout.

"Help!" Mike yells.

You stop to listen. An owl hoots. A twig snaps. But you don't hear anyone call back.

Carla blows the whistle again. You shout some more, but Mike hushes you.

He points in the direction you came from. "Look," he says.

There's an orange glow along the horizon. That means fire. It's usually best to stay in one spot, but a forest fire is dangerous. If it's close enough to see, you should keep moving.

"Come on," you tell your friends.

You walk in the direction away from the fire. Your friends follow.

After a few minutes, Carla says, "Stop. I think I hear water."

"It's the river," Mike adds.

You follow the sound. You and your friends come to the river's bank. You look across its black surface and see trees on the other side.

"How deep is the water?" asks Mike.

"Not very," Carla says. "We waded into it last year. The water only went up to my chest."

If you cross the river, you will be safely away from the fire. But should you cross it? It's dark out, and you can't see very well. Plus, water can be just as deadly as fire.

What will you do?

Cross the river.

Don't cross the river.

Cross the river: You tell your friends to wade across. You take the first step into the water. It's cold. You take another step. Your foot slides across a slimy rock, and you almost fall. This seems pretty dangerous. You shouldn't do it.

Don't cross the river: You tell your friends that it's too dangerous to cross the river. Good choice! You could slip and fall. You also don't know if the water is deeper than last year. And you don't know how strong the current is.

"Maybe we can walk beside the river," you say. "Mike, do you still have a park map?"

"Yes," he says. "It's in my pocket."

He pulls out the map. He unfolds it, so you can all look. The river forms the western border of the park. At one point, it comes very close to the trail. It also leads to the park beach, near the visitor center.

Now that you know where you are, it's safe to find your way out of the woods.

7. Scary Noises

You lead your friends, but you move slowly. You only have a flashlight. So it's hard to see where you're walking. When there's a log in your path, you shine the light on it. You don't want your friends to trip and get hurt.

Lots of bushes and shrubs grow along the riverbank. Sometimes, you have to force your way through them. Other times, you have to leave the riverbank and walk around them. You listen for the water. It helps to find your way back to the river.

Every once in a while, Mike asks to stop. "Shine the flashlight on the map," he says. He studies the map for a few seconds.

"Do you know where we are?" Carla asks.

He shakes his head. "Not exactly," he answers. "We could still be a mile from the beach."

Then you hear . . . *Ah-rooooo!*

You jump at the sound. Your body starts to shiver. Your friends look around wildly.

"What was that?" Carla screeches. "A coyote?"

"A wolf," Mike whispers.

It's dark. You can hardly see anything. And now wolves are howling in the woods.

Ah-ah-ah-rooooo!

The wolf sounds closer. Your friends' eyes are wide with fear. You all huddle close to each other.

"Wolves hunt in packs," Mike says. "There's more than one of them out there."

Ah-rooooo!

You imagine wild animals darting between the trees. It's a scary thought. And you're also worried about your friends. They're even more scared than you are.

You need to remain calm for your friends. You'll have to tell them what to do.

You could ask your friends to huddle together and keep quiet. Maybe the wolves won't know you're there. They just might walk right by you.

Or maybe you should make some noise. That will tell the wolves exactly where you are. But it could also scare them away.

What will you tell your friends to do?

Stay quiet.

Make noise.

Stay quiet: You tell your friends to stay quiet. But then you remember something your dad told you. Animals are usually only dangerous if you surprise them. It would be better to make some noise, so the wolves know you're there.

Make noise: You tell your friends that it's best to make some noise. Most animals stay away from humans. If you make noise, they'll know where you are. They will try to avoid you.

You and your friends start talking loudly.

"I wish we weren't lost!" Mike shouts.

"Me, too!" Carla says.

"Someone will find us!" you add.

"I hope so!" Mike yells.

"Me, too!" Carla booms again.

The next time you hear the wolves, they sound farther away.

"How long do we have to talk like this?" Mike shouts.

"I don't know!" you answer.

"We could sing a song!" Carla yells.

"Now that would really scare the wolves away!" Mike jokes.

8. Hungry

Your throat gets sore. You and your friends stop shouting, and you listen. Crickets chirp. Owls hoot. The wind blows. But when you hear a wolf howl, it's far in the distance. You breathe a sigh of relief.

Then it begins to rain.

"Could this night get any worse?" Carla moans.

"Hey, it's just rain," you say. "It's good news for the fire. And we have ponchos in the survival kit."

That bit of news brightens Mike's mood. He even smiles as he slips the poncho over his head.

But Carla still frowns. She puts on her poncho. Then she crosses her arms under it.

"What's wrong?" you ask.

"I'm hungry," she complains. "We should have grabbed our snacks. I could use some trail mix."

"There wasn't enough time," you say.

"I know. I'm just starving. And I get cranky when I'm hungry."

"Hey, look at these berries," Mike says. "Maybe we can eat them."

You shine the flashlight at the bush beside Mike. It's hard to tell what type of berries they are. But they look blue with a smooth, shiny skin.

"I think they're blueberries," says Carla.

"They'd make a great snack," says Mike.

You're hungry too. All the excitement and running has caused your stomach to grumble. And you don't know how long you'll be in the woods.

You need energy to keep going, so you need a snack. But you aren't sure about the berries. They kind of look like blueberries, but what if they're not?

What will you do?

Eat the berries.

Don't eat the berries.

Eat the berries: You start picking the berries. You collect a handful. They look delicious. But are they really blueberries? You know that some berries can be harmful and make you sick. You don't know for sure what these are. You shouldn't eat them.

Don't eat the berries: Your parents have a book about wild berries. It says not to eat any wild fruit unless you know what it is. Some berries can make you sick. To be safe, you better not eat these berries.

"I'm not sure these are blueberries," you say. "We better not eat them."

"But I'm hungry," Carla whines.

"And we're all wet," Mike moans.

"Come on," you tell your friends. "Let's keep following the river. Maybe we'll get to the visitor center soon. They'll have food there."

9. Calls for Help

Once you start walking, your friends seem to be in better moods. It takes their minds off the rain.

As you're walking, you hear something. Not an animal but a person. You tell your friends to stop. You listen.

"Help!" a man's voice calls.

It sounds far away, somewhere behind you.

"That could be my dad," you say.

Slowly, you start moving toward the voice.

"Mom?" you shout. "Dad?"

The only response is another distant, "Help!"

It's still raining, but the fire probably isn't out yet. You're worried about returning to the area.

"What should we do?" Carla asks.

"Is it safe?" says Mike.

You scan the horizon. You don't see the orange glow of flames. You don't smell any smoke. There doesn't seem to be any danger at the moment.

"Help!" you hear the voice again.

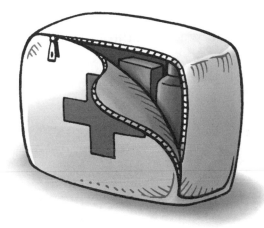

"Is anyone there?" a second voice yells. It sounds like a boy.

You're pretty sure that the people in trouble aren't your parents. Maybe they're the ones from the third campsite. They would've run from the fire, too.

"We have the survival kit," Carla says. "If they're hurt, we could help them."

There's no fire or smoke in that direction. It would probably be safe to help. But part of you is afraid. You could get lost again. And a fire could still be burning deep in the woods.

What will you do?

Help them.

Don't help.

Help them: You decide to help. After all, if you were in trouble, you would want people to help you. And you still have your survival kit with the whistle. Even if you get lost again, hopefully you can attract help by making enough noise.

– – – – – – – – – – – – –

Don't help: You don't think you should help. But the voices keep calling. The people could be hurt. Carla and Mike stare in the direction of the voices. You should probably help them, after all.

"Let's go to them," you tell your friends.

They seem to like this idea, especially Mike.

"We'll be heroes," he says. "Just like Spider-Man!"

You head off in the direction of the voices.

10. People in Need

The rain stops, but the forest is still dark and wet. Leaves squish under your feet. Branches slap your arms.

"Where are you?" you shout.

"Here!" the man replies.

"This way!" yells the boy.

You can't really tell where they are. But it sounds like you're getting closer.

"Are you okay?" you shout back. You're worried that the people could be hurt.

The boy replies, "We're okay."

"But I can't walk," the man shouts.

Now you're worried. What will you do when you find them? You're not a doctor.

You step over a fallen tree. Some of its branches have been singed by fire. You touch them. The bark is cool and wet, even where it was charred. Hopefully that means the fire is out.

You remember the campfire from last night. Even when the coals were black on top, they were still hot underneath. You will need to be careful.

Slowly, you and your friends wind your way through the woods. You see more burned trees. Most of them have no leaves on their lower branches.

You're thankful that it rained.

Suddenly, you step onto a trail. Down the trail, you see the boy and man.

They sit on the ground. The man looks about your parents' age. The boy is a bit older than you. You guess that they are father and son.

They are shivering. Their clothes are soaked. And they're only wearing t-shirts and shorts. You take off your poncho and hand it to the boy. Carla hands hers to the man.

Scrapes and cuts cover the boy's arms and legs. He probably got them while running through the woods. The man also has scrapes on his arms. Worse, he has one of his shoes off. His ankle looks swollen.

You have the survival kit. There are bandages and other supplies inside. You could treat the man's injuries now.

But he needs a doctor. And the sooner he gets one, the better. You could ignore the strangers' injuries and help them out of the woods.

What will you do?

Treat their injuries.

Help them out of the woods.

Treat their injuries: You unzip the survival kit. There are bandages and ointments for cuts. You apply ointments to the boy's scratches. Carla helps the man. You aren't sure how much it really helps, but they thank you.

Help them out of the woods: You and Carla try to help the man up, but he is bigger and heavier than you. He takes one step, and the three of you almost fall over. You might make his ankle worse. You should make a different choice.

"They're still shivering," Mike says.

"What should we do?" Carla asks.

"We have matches in the survival kit," you say. "We can start a fire."

After the scare of the forest fire, you're a little frightened by this idea. But you are also cold.

11. To the Visitor Center

Carla gathers some dry sticks and fallen branches. She breaks them apart. She hands them to you before going to gather some more.

You create a small area clear of any twigs or leaves. That's where you arrange the broken branches into a pyramid. You tuck some leaves into the middle of the pyramid.

It takes several tries. Everything is kind of damp. But you get a small fire going. Carefully, you feed the fire more twigs. The boy and the man huddle near it. The fire warms all of you.

Mike studies the map. "I think I know where we are," he says.

He brings the map to you. He shines the flashlight on it and points to it. "That's the river," he explains. "We walked east when we heard the calls for help."

"How do you know we went east?" Carla asks.

He says. "We couldn't go west without crossing the river. By walking away from it, we went east."

Mikes points to another spot on the map. "I bet the trail we're on is the same one we took to our campsite," he explains.

You look around. Nothing is familiar, but it's dark. You can't tell if he's right or wrong, but you trust him.

"North takes us to our campsite," Mike says.

"Then south takes us to the visitor center," you add. It's the best news you've heard all night.

Normally, if you're lost, you should stay in one place. But now that you know where you are, you can send one of your friends for help. Who should go, Carla or Mike?

Carla is faster than Mike. And you're sure she has the energy to get to the visitor center.

Mike might also be a good choice. He's smart. He can read a map better than anyone. He's the one who figured out where you are.

Who will you send?

Carla

Mike

Carla: You ask Carla to go for help. She nods. You give her the flashlight, and Mike hands her the map. She seems nervous. You can tell she's worried about getting lost. Maybe you should ask Mike to go instead.

Mike: You ask Mike if he'll go for help. He nods eagerly. You give him the flashlight, and he has the map. You know that he's good at finding his way. You feel like you've made a good choice.

"I think we're only a half mile from the end of the trail," he says. "I should be back soon."

"We'll blow the whistle every few minutes, so you know where we are," you say.

You watch him step out of the firelight. The light from his flashlight shines through the trees. It grows smaller and smaller. Then finally it winks out.

"I hope he'll be okay," you say to Carla.

"If anyone can find the way," Carla says, "Mike can."

12. Smart Choices

Tweet! Carla blows the whistle.

You listen. You hear nothing.

Tweet! Carla blows the whistle again.

It feels like hours have passed since Mike left. You're worried about him. But you know that he's good with maps.

"It's our fault," the boy says. "We caused the forest fire."

"It's all my fault," says the man. "I let our campfire burn even after we went to bed."

"Were you in the site next to us?" you ask.

"Yes, that was us," the boy says.

"This is our first camping trip together," the man adds.

You're angry. They caused a lot of damage. They ruined your camping trip, too. Yet you feel sorry for them. They weren't as prepared as you.

Tweet! Carla blows the whistle one more time.

"We're coming," a distant voice calls.

You and Carla stand at the edge of the firelight, waiting. You hear people stomping through the woods. Next, you see a ball of light shining between the trees. Finally, Mike steps out of the dark. A park ranger is with him.

"Is everyone alright?" the ranger asks.

"We are," says Carla.

"My dad hurt his ankle," the boy says.

74

"Where are my parents?" you ask.

"They're at the visitor center with another park ranger," Mike answers.

The park ranger helps the injured man stand up. You hear the man grunt.

"Is this everyone?" the ranger asks.

You nod.

"Okay, let's head back," he says. "Lucky for us, the fire wasn't very big. I think the rain put it out. But let's not take any chances."

He turns to Mike. "Can you lead us?" he asks.

Mike smiles. "I can," he says.

You and Carla follow him. But you have to walk slowly. The park ranger helps the man along.

Eventually you reach the trail's end. There are lights flashing from several fire engines. All the other campers crowd around the visitor center.

As you step out of the woods, your parents call to you. You run to them, and they hug you tightly.

"We were so worried," your dad says.

"How did you survive out there in the woods?" your mom asks.

You smile and say, "By making smart choices."

CONGRATULATIONS!

You made good decisions and saved your friends from the

Camping Tips

1. **Bring the right clothes.** Always bring clothes for cold weather, like sweatshirts and long pants, and rainy weather, such as a poncho.

2. **Store food away from your tent.** This is also true of anything with a scent, like toothpaste and perfume. The scent of food will attract animals. So store it in a car, or hang it from a tree.

3. **Make sure someone is always watching your fire.** One spark can ignite dry grass or leaves near your fire pit. And always put out your fire with water before going to bed at night.

4. **If you're lost, stay put.** Moving around will make it harder for people to find you. There are only two reasons to move from your location: 1) you're in danger, or 2) you know where you are.

Survival Kit

Here's a list of helpful items to have in your survival kit:

1. First-aid items, like bandages and ointments
2. Waterproof matches
3. A whistle
4. A compass
5. A map of the area where you're camping
6. Snack bars
7. Water bottle and water purification tablets
8. Emergency rain poncho
9. Utility knife
10. Rope or strong string

About the Author

Blake Hoena grew up in central Wisconsin. In his youth, he wrote stories about robots conquering the moon and trolls lumbering around in the woods behind his parents' house. The fact that the trolls were hunting for little boys had nothing to do with Blake's pesky brothers.

Later, he moved to Minnesota to pursue a Master of Fine Arts degree in Creative Writing from Minnesota State University, Mankato.

Since graduating, Blake has written more than fifty books for children. Currently he is working on more Choose Your Path books. For more about Blake, visit www.bahoena.com.